Story by **RUTH KRAUSS**

THE HAPPY EGG

Pictures by **CROCKETT JOHNSON**

HarperCollins*Publishers*

The Happy Egg

Library of Congress Cataloging-in-Publication Data
Krauss, Ruth.
The happy egg. / Story by Ruth Krauss ; pictures by Crockett Johnson.
Summary: A bird hatches from its egg and learns to fly.
ISBN 0-06-076005-2 — ISBN 0-06-076006-0 (lib. bdg.)
[1. Birds—Fiction.]
PZ10.3.K87Har5 2005 72186887
[E] CIP
AC

Typography by Neil Swaab
1 2 3 4 5 6 7 8 9 10
❖
First HarperCollins Edition
Originally published by Scholastic Inc., in 1967.

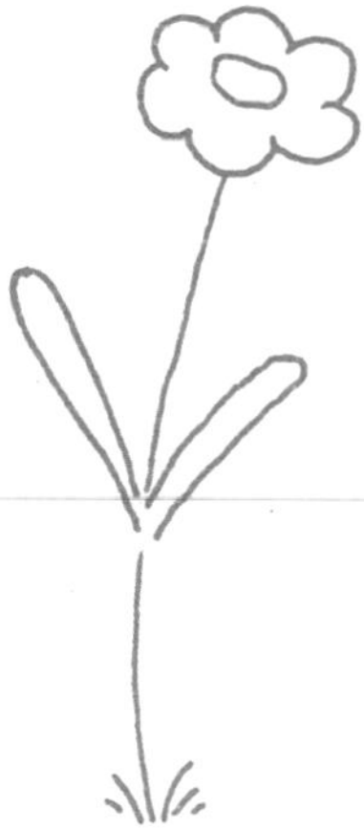

There was a little little bird.

It was just born.
It still was an egg.

It couldn't walk.
It couldn't sing.
It couldn't fly.

It could just get sat on.

So it got sat on
and sat on

and sat on
and sat on

and sat on
and sat on
and sat on

and sat on.

And one day,

peep

POP! Out it came.

It could walk.

It could sing.

It could

fly.

It could someday sit on
other happy eggs.

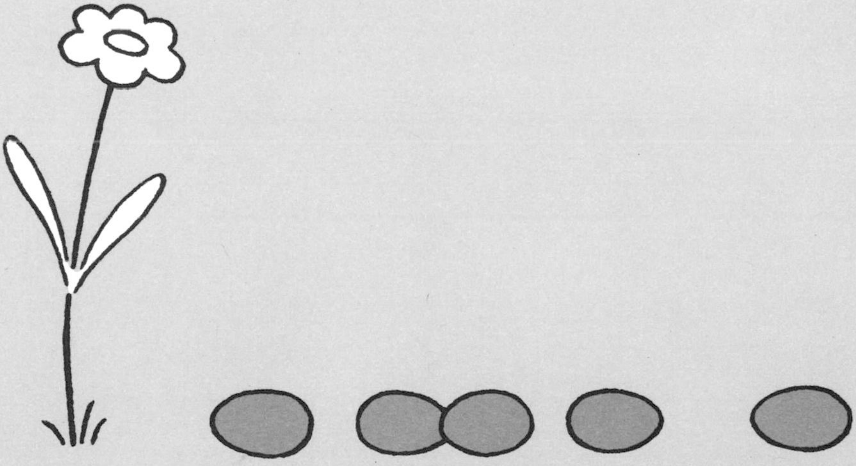